For Gabe and Rafi and Tom – for ever and always,
And for Ben – my sunshine on a rainy day – S.P-H.

For Mike and Cal – thank you for your love and support come rain or shine! A.F.

HODDER CHILDREN'S BOOKS

First published in 2016 by Hodder and Stoughton
This paperback edition published in 2017

Hodder Children's Books
An imprint of Hachette Children's Group
Part of Hodder and Stoughton
Carmelite House, 50 Victoria Embankment
London EC4Y 0DZ

A catalogue record of this book is available from the British Library.

ISBN: 978 1 444 92215 8
10 9 8 7 6 5 4 3 2 1

Printed in China

An Hachette UK Company
www.hachette.co.uk

h
Hodder
Children's
Books

My Hand to Hold

Smriti Prasadam-Halls & Alison Friend

I love you when the days are bright,
And everything you do feels right.

But when you make your world a mess,
I don't **love you** any less.

I love you

in the dazzling sun,

When everything

we do seems fun.

But when you have to shout and yell,
I love you at those times as well.

I love you as the leaves turn gold,
When you're feeling brave and bold.

But on the days when you feel shy,

I'll help you hold your head up high.

I love you when the snow lies deep,
And all the world is fast asleep.

And when the days are bleak and cold,

You've always got my hand to hold.

I love you right through all your days,

I love you in so many ways.

Through storms

and sun

and snow and rain,

Right back till spring
is here again!

As every day begins anew,
I love you strong, I love you true.

For all the things you say and do. . .

For everything that makes you YOU.

Little One

Jo Weaver

MIJ KELLY · GERRY TURLEY

LOVE
Matters Most

Good Night, I Love You

Caroline Jayne Church

Love this book?
Try these heart-warming stories:

A
Recipe
for Bedtime

PETER BENTLY & SARAH MASSINI

WHO puts the ANIMALS to BED?

MIJ KELLY and HOLLY CLIFTON-BROWN

For fun activities, further
information and to order, visit
www.hodderchildrens.co.uk